Ellie ☆ Sandall

EVERYBUNNY
Count!

4...

5...   6...   7...

h
Hodder
Children's
Books

Fox and bunnies like to play,
all together, every day.

Playing **hide-and-seek** today...

EVERYBUNNY COUNT!

1 2 3 4 5

Take your places, everyone.
Ready or not, here we come!

The search for fox has just begun.
Everybunny count to ONE!

We found some birds, away they flew.
Everybunny count to TWO!

We've spotted something in the tree.
Everybunny count to THREE!

Tiny creatures in my paw.
Everybunny count to FOUR!

Check the water, in we dive.
Everybunny count to FIVE!

Look who's hiding in the sticks.
Everybunny count to SIX!

Carrots! We're in bunny heaven.
Everybunny count to **SEVEN**!

Where's that fox? It's getting late.
Everybunny count to EIGHT!

Sleepy bunnies in a line.

Everybunny count to NINE!

Through a bush, behind some rocks.

Everybunny look...

Now take a peek inside the den.

EVERYBUNNY COUNT...

Foxes, bunnies,

one to ten.

Let's play **hide-and-seek** again!